Ark Adventures

Noah and his wife think a flood might be coming, so they have built a big boat called the Ark. They are sailing around the world to rescue the animals before it starts to rain.

Let's all go on an animal adventure!

For Owen Chesney
S.G.

For Amy
A.P.

Reading Consultant: Prue Goodwin, Lecturer in literacy and children's books

ORCHARD BOOKS
338 Euston Road, London NW1 3BH
Orchard Books Australia
Level 17/207 Kent Street, Sydney, NSW 2000

First published in 2011
First paperback publication in 2012

ISBN 978 1 40830 560 7 (hardback)
ISBN 978 1 40830 568 3 (paperback)

A CIP catalogue record for this book is available from the British Library.

1 3 5 7 9 10 8 6 4 2 (hardback)
1 3 5 7 9 10 8 6 4 2 (paperback)

Printed in China

Orchard Books is a division of Hachette Children's Books,
an Hachette UK company.

Cheeky
Chimpanzees!

Written by Sally Grindley

Illustrated by Alex Paterson

ORCHARD BOOKS

"There's a sign ahead, Noah," said Mrs Noah. "Can you read what it says?"

Noah picked up his
binoculars. "Africa,"
he read.

"How exciting!" said
Mrs Noah.

"Which animals will we find this time?" said Mrs Noah.
Noah looked in their *Big Book of Animals*. "It says there are chimpanzees," he said.
"What a funny name!" said Mrs Noah. "What are they like?"

"They scream a lot . . . and they like tea parties," Noah read.

"Ooh, good," said Mrs Noah. "I can make fairy cakes."

"Ooh, good," said Noah. "I love fairy cakes."

They sailed the Ark along a river
until they could go no further.

Noah went below deck.

He came back wearing earmuffs.

"I'll find the chimpanzees while you get the tea party ready," he said. "With these earmuffs on, I won't be able to hear the chimpanzees scream."

"Clever Noah," said Mrs Noah.

"Shall I make jelly?"

"Did you say I'm smelly?"
said Noah.

"I asked if you wanted
jelly," said Mrs Noah.

"Not at all," said Noah. "But can we have jelly, please?"

Mrs Noah rolled her eyes.

"Silly Noah!" she said.

Noah stepped ashore and set off through the rainforest. "It's very quiet in here," he said to himself. "I wonder why the birds aren't singing?"

Just then, Noah
saw a black shape
swinging through
the treetops.

"Is that a
chimpanzee?"
he wondered.
"I can't hear any
screaming."

13

Suddenly, something hit him on the head.

"Ouch!" he cried. "What was that?"

Something hit him on the nose.

"Eeek!" he cried.

"What was that?"

Two chimpanzees were swinging
backwards and forwards through the
trees. One of them picked a fruit and
threw it at Noah.

"Hey, stop that!" cried Noah. "I've come to invite you to a tea party."

The chimpanzees leapt to the ground. One of them ran up to Noah and hugged him.

"That's nice," said Noah.

The other one picked up a stick and poked it into an anthill.

"That's clever," said Noah.

The chimpanzee pulled the stick out.
It was covered in ants! He offered it
to Noah.

Noah shook his head. "No, thank
you," he said. "I'm not very keen on
ants."

The first chimpanzee picked a nut
and held it out to him.

Noah shook his head. "No, thank you," he said. "I'm allergic to nuts."

The chimpanzee ran away and came back with a very smelly fruit.

"No, thank you," said Noah. "I don't want to spoil our tea party. We're having fairy cakes and jelly!"

The chimpanzees screamed with excitement, but Noah couldn't hear them.

"You don't sound very excited," said Noah. "Don't you like tea parties?"

23

The chimpanzees
began to skip along
the ground, pulling
Noah behind them.

"Don't go so
fast!" he cried,
trying to keep up.

24

As soon as the chimpanzees saw the Ark, they leapt up and down and screamed loudly.

Mrs Noah waved at them.

"Our book was right," she called to Noah. "They are very noisy."

"I'm not lazy!" argued Noah.

"No," said Mrs Noah, rolling her eyes again. "I said they're very *noisy*."

"By the way, our book was wrong," said Noah. "Chimpanzees are as quiet as mice."

The chimpanzees ran up the
gangplank and hugged Mrs Noah.

"Welcome on board," she smiled.

When Noah walked up the gangplank, one of the chimpanzees pulled his earmuffs off and screamed loudly.

Noah stuck his fingers in his ears. "Goodness me!" he cried. "No wonder it was so quiet. I had forgotten I had earmuffs on."

The chimpanzees screamed again.
"I think they're hungry," said
Mrs Noah. "Let's have our party."

"Ooh, yes," said Noah. He picked
up a fairy cake. "I love fairy cakes,
don't you?"

The chimpanzees grabbed the cakes
and jelly and stuffed their mouths full!
Mrs Noah smiled. "That's one way
to keep them quiet," she said.
"Peace at last," said Noah.

SALLY GRINDLEY · ALEX PATERSON

Crazy Chameleons!	978 1 40830 562 1
Giant Giraffes!	978 1 40830 563 8
Too-slow Tortoises!	978 1 40830 564 5
Kung Fu Kangaroos!	978 1 40830 565 2
Playful Penguins!	978 1 40830 566 9
Pesky Sharks!	978 1 40830 567 6
Cheeky Chimpanzees!	978 1 40830 568 3
Hungry Bears!	978 1 40830 569 0

All priced at £4.99

Orchard Books are available from all good bookshops, or can be
ordered from our website: www.orchardbooks.co.uk,
or telephone 01235 827702, or fax 01235 827703.